Elizabeth and Larry

SIMON & SCHUSTER BOOKS FOR YOUNG READERS
Simon & Schuster Building
Rockefeller Center
1230 Avenue of the Americas
New York, New York 10020

10 9 8 7 6 5 4 3 2 1

(pbk) 10 9 8 7 6 5 4 3 2 1

Library of Congress Cataloging-in-Publication Data
Sadler, Marilyn.
Elizabeth and Larry / by Marilyn Sadler; illustrated by Roger Bollen. p.   cm.
Summary: Elizabeth and Larry are contented best friends until Larry
is scorned by neighbors for being an alligator.
[1. Friendship—Fiction.   2. Prejudices—Fiction.   3. Alligators—Fiction.]
1. Bollen, Roger, ill.   II. Title.   PZ7.S1239E1   1990   [E]-dc20   89-11552   CIP   AC

ISBN 0-671-69189-9   ISBN 0-671-77817-X (pbk)

Elizabeth and Larry

By Marilyn Sadler
Illustrated by Roger Bollen

Simon & Schuster Books for Young Readers
Published by Simon & Schuster
New York • London • Toronto • Sydney • Tokyo • Singapore

ELIZABETH and LARRY were old friends.
Elizabeth was sixty-two, and Larry was
pushing forty.

Elizabeth met Larry for the first time many years ago. He was delivered to her by mistake with the box of oranges she ordered from Florida.

Elizabeth decided to keep Larry, and she gave him a room above the garage. She put the oranges in the refrigerator.

Larry loved his new home. His only complaint
had to do with the size of the pool.

Every day Elizabeth and Larry went
walking. Larry was always drawn to the zoo.
He was fascinated by the unusual exhibits.

On sunny days they went to the beach.
Larry taught Elizabeth how to float. He also
taught her how to dive for fish.

Everywhere they went, people stared at them.
Elizabeth thought it was because everyone wanted
a friend like Larry. Then one day she found out
it was because no one liked Larry.

This was the first time Larry realized
he was different. Up until then, he had
assumed he looked like Elizabeth.

So as the years passed by, Elizabeth and Larry spent less time out and more time alone at home together.

They talked for hours over tea and told
each other things they had never told
anyone.

They loved to play cards. Although
Elizabeth preferred old maid, Larry's
game was poker.

Larry was a big help around the house,
too. There was nothing he loved more than
vacuuming. Sometimes he dumped potting
soil on the rug on purpose, so that he could
clean it up.

And when Elizabeth had knitting to do,
Larry held the yarn. It was the least he could
do in return for the leg warmers.

Whenever Elizabeth and Larry did go out,
Larry went in disguise. He did not like
wearing Elizabeth's clothes, but people
seemed to like old ladies better than they
did alligators.

Once, while they were out walking, a man
tried to take Larry's pocketbook.

But he changed his mind.

Then one day, some of Elizabeth's relatives
came to visit. She had not seen them for
many years. Larry was surprised to see how
much they looked like Elizabeth.

They were very nice to Larry. But Larry did not feel like part of the family. He wanted to look like Elizabeth too.

After that, Larry was not himself. He
boiled water for tea, but forgot the tea bags.

He went out without his hat or
his pocketbook.

He didn't even try to get rid of the old maid.

Elizabeth had never seen Larry so sad. But she had known Larry for many years, and she knew what was wrong. Larry was tired of being different. He wanted to be with alligators.

So it was quite sadly decided that Larry would
return to Florida. Elizabeth took Larry to the
airport and bought him a one-way ticket home.

Everyone was staring at them when they said good-bye.

After that, Elizabeth was not herself.
Every day she sat at her window and
waited for letters from Larry. Larry
wrote to her often, but it was not the
same. Even his phone calls did not
comfort her.

Everyone who knew Elizabeth had never
seen her look worse.
"What you need is a cat," they said.

But what Elizabeth really needed was
to be with Larry.

So one day Elizabeth sold her house and bought a one-way ticket to Florida. She also bought some mints, and a magazine to read on the plane.

When Elizabeth arrived in Florida, Larry was there to greet her. They agreed they would never part again.

Elizabeth loved her new home.
Her only complaint had to do with
the size of the pool.

It wasn't quite large enough.